So What?

Written by Heather Gemmen
Illustrated by Luciano Lagares

Equipping Kids for Life!

A Faith Parenting Guide can be found on page 32.

Everything was perfect
until Katie came around.

She stomped on my new robot—
so I pushed her to the ground.

3

I heard Kate call to mommy
(for the twenty-millionth time).

I turned back to my robot
to forget about my crime.

When Mommy came I vroomed real loud so she would go away.

Vroo-oom!

But she still sat down next to me.
"I have some things to say."

"The Bible says that even kids
are known for how they act."
I shrugged and said, "So what?" to her.
"My robot was attacked."

9

"I'm glad you asked the question,"
my mommy said to me.

"'So what?' means 'What will happen now?' Wouldn't you agree?"

"Come on," she said and grabbed my hand.
"Pretend you are a spy.
You and I will look for clues.
We'll give it a good try."

Now spying is a lot of fun—
I'm stealthy and I'm sly.
But mom spied on a dying plant!
I just could not see why.

"See that plant?" she said to me.
It hardly looked suspicious.

"Mom, it's plain and brown and gross. It's not strange or vicious."

"Look for clues to tell me why that plant is almost dead."

I snuck up close and touched the dirt. "It's dry," I wisely said.

"Ah ha! 'So what' is answered then!"
my mom said with a wink.

"How about that sandwich there? What happened do you think?"

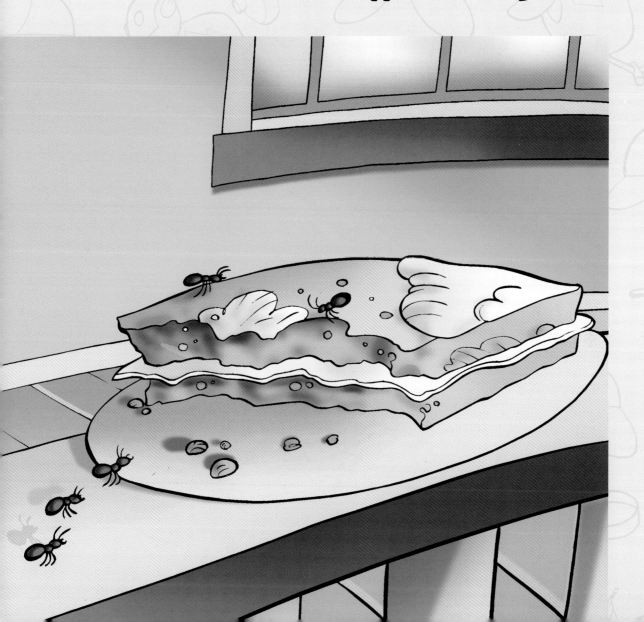

"I left it out. I'm sorry, Mom—"
But Mom held up a hand.
"'So what' is what's important now.
Please try to understand."

I watched Mom drop a chunk of ice
into a patch of sun.
I told her that the ice would melt.
"I know! This is so fun!"

"And if I tossed this airplane—
what would happen then?"
"Don't throw it, Mom, 'cause it would break!"
"A consequence again!"

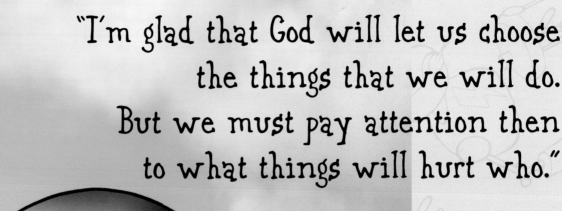

"I'm glad that God will let us choose
the things that we will do.
But we must pay attention then
to what things will hurt who."

I looked at Kate who seemed so sad.
I didn't wonder why.

"I'm sorry that I pushed you, Kate. It's good I was a spy."

So What?

Life Issue: I want my children to understand the consequences of their actions.

Spiritual Building Block: Responsibility

Do the following activities to help your children become accountable for their choices:

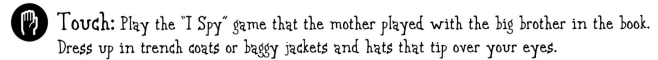

Touch: Play the "I Spy" game that the mother played with the big brother in the book. Dress up in trench coats or baggy jackets and hats that tip over your eyes.

Search for left-out cups of milk that have gone sour and doors that haven't been closed along with the bug that got inside as a result.

Also look for positive things like being able to find a toy right away because it was put back in its place and markers that still draw beautiful colors because the lids were put back on them.

Reiterate to your children that God wants them to make the right decisions and that good choices end in first-rate results.

Get all of These Great Tough Stuff Titles for Your Child!

Heather Gemmen

Growing up can be a hard thing. That's why we created the Tough Stuff for Kids Series! The delightful art and pleasant rhyme of these books make reading these stories enjoyable for young children. They will want to read the stories over and over again while parents will love the spiritual lessons and help for the Tough Stuff kids face.

8 x 8   Paperback   36P each

0-78144-035-1

0-78144-036-X

0-78144-033-5

0-78143-853-5

0-78143-851-9

0-78143-852-7

0-78143-854-3

Order Your Copies Today!
Order Online: www.cookministries.com
Phone: 1-800-323-7543
Or Visit your Local Christian Bookstore

The Word at Work Around the World

What would you do if you wanted to share God's love with children on the streets of your city? That's the dilemma David C. Cook faced in 1870's Chicago. His answer was to create literature that would capture children's hearts.

Out of those humble beginnings grew a worldwide ministry that has used literature to proclaim God's love and disciple generation after generation. Cook Communications Ministries is committed to personal discipleship—to helping people of all ages learn God's Word, embrace his salvation, walk in his ways, and minister in his name.

Faith Kidz, RiverOak, Honor, Life Journey, Victor, NextGen . . . every time you purchase a book produced by Cook Communications Ministries, you not only meet a vital personal need in your life or in the life of someone you love, but you're also a part of ministering to José in Colombia, Humberto in Chile, Gousa in India, or Lidiane in Brazil. You help make it possible for a pastor in China, a child in Peru, or a mother in West Africa to enjoy a life-changing book. And because you helped, children and adults around the world are learning God's Word and walking in his ways.

Thank you for your partnership in helping to disciple the world. May God bless you with the power of his Word in your life.

For more information about our international ministries,
visit www.ccmi.org.